THE HUNGUR

CHRONICLES

Walpurgisnacht
2024

Edited by:
TERRIE LEIGH RELF
&
ROBERT BELLAM

THE STAFF OF THE HUNGUR CHRONICLES

EDITOR: Terrie Leigh Relf
ASSOCIATE EDITOR: Robert Bellam
WEBMASTER: H David Blalock

Cover art "Forest Vampire" by Sandy DeLuca
Cover design by Marcia Borell

Vol. III, No. 1   May 2024
The Hungur Chronicles is published semiannually on the 1st day of May and November in the United States of America by Hiraeth Publishing, P.O. Box 1248, Tularosa, NM, 88352. Copyright 2024 by Hiraeth Publishing. All rights revert to authors and artists upon publication except as noted in selected individual contracts. Nothing may be reproduced in whole or in part without written permission from the authors and artists. Any similarity between places and persons mentioned in the fiction or semi-fiction and real places or persons living or dead is coincidental. Writers and artists guidelines are available online at www.hiraethsffh.com. Guidelines are also available upon request from Hiraeth Publishing, P.O. Box 1248, Tularosa, NM, 88352, if request is accompanied by a self-addressed #10 envelope with a first-class US stamp. Editor: Tyree Campbell.

Support the First Amendment and the Small Independent Publishers! Remember, our right to publish is your right to read.

Contents

Features
6   Editors' Notes

Stories
7   Lamia by Francis W. Alexander
18 Goody Gumdrop by Stephen McQuiggan
33 Phantoms by Eddie Spohn
48 Two of a Kind by Steve Burford

Flash Fiction
30 Necking by Christopher Ananias

Poetry
17 A Good Meal by Guy Belleranti
29 Me That Was by Tyree Campbell
59 Amalthea by Terrie Leigh Relf

Sabit the Sumerian

a novella by Tyree Campbell
inspired by the Epic of Gilgamesh!

Cursed and banished to the dung-filled streets of Uruk by the king for whom she was once a companion, Sabit must now sell herself in order to survive. Near starving, and bearing the mark of the *lillu*, or vampire, she is plagued by dreams of the ancient ones who dwell beyond the mountains of Elam.

Sabit meets a girl around her own age, a kind girl with brilliant blue eyes, who asks what no other woman has ever asked: "What are you selling?" That night, Sabit's new friend comes to her in a dream, asking for that which cannot be taken, but freely given. The girl is Shala, Daughter of Ereshkigal, Goddess of the Underworld. Vampire.

Thousands of years pass. One night, Sabit, now known as Adrienne Bouchard, meets a man in a park, and her life is irrevocably changed once more. His name is Ian Cullen, a recently widowed archaeologist, with a young daughter auspiciously named Shala.

When the Daughter of Ereshkigal returns, she commands Adrienne to make a choice: Kill or turn Ian and his daughter. How will she choose? Will Adrienne sacrifice herself for two humans? Are they nothing but cattle after all?

https://www.hiraethsffh.com/product-page/sabit-the-sumerian-by-tyree-campbell

A Note from Your Editors,
Terrie Leigh Relf and Robert Bellam

Hungur Chronicles, Issue Five

May 1, 2024

A Note from Your Editors . . .

Welcome to the fifth issue of *Hungur Chronicles!* We certainly hope you enjoy reading this issue as much as we did curating it. Here's to vampires of all ilks, the stranger the better. We have some wonderfully quirky and literary tales for you—including extra-terrestrial jaunts.

(And yes, the King's English is welcomed here.)

—Terrie Leigh Relf, Lead Editor

—Robert Bellam, Co-Editor

Acknowledgements:

Amalthea was originally published in 2016 in Space & Time

Lamia
Francis W. Alexander

Day 1

Looking into the sky, I see the mighty armada with its silver skin gleaming in the sunlight as it moves through and then past the amethyst clouds. I had warned the company not to come here. My words of caution were futile. G&P Corporation needs this planet's lanthanum and is determined to get it at any cost. And since we're "infected", that leaves us expendable.

We rush to the caves for protection. The distant explosions remind me of the day we arrived here.

***

As the door to our transport opened on that dreary arrival day, I heard the drums. I was so into the rhythm of the beat that I was tempted to break out into a dance.

Thick fluffballs, the color of lilacs, joined in the mystery party. They refused to release rain and denied the sun its entrance. Our ship had missed the projected landing area we named Lan Mountain by about ten meters. Everything below was purple, purple, purple, green, and red. It was mostly vegetation. Although not like the Earth with its display of major cities and towering skyscrapers, I later found out that this planet wasn't primitive either.

We touched down on a large sandy clearing surrounded by bushes and shrubs. With oxygen at a safe level and no apparent pathogens, a party of seven, including myself and an android, left the ship. Although we were confident our cyborg doctors and their android staff were prepared to treat us in any emergency, just to be on the safe side, we still wore our helmets.

"Look! A welcoming committee," said Paula Ahoka. Decked in green robes and silky headdresses, the natives stood between two trees about fifty meters from us. The odd thing about them was that their formation consisted of the tallest being in the middle and going down in size to the smallest on both ends.

Look. A new delicacy, I thought of the natives as saying. Yes, dark humor is on my resume.

The locals and the surrounding area were bathed in a mauve mist, so I figured that we must have arrived in the morning.

"Don't touch anything," I said over the mic.

As we drew near the aboriginals, I noticed the odd-looking plants surrounding us. They could be described as the sunflower's cousin. Instead of a disk floret, the plants had a navy-blue carpel surrounded by yellow silky hairs.

"Those people are freaking me out," Yolonda Sanchez said as she grabbed my arm. The natives' gawking gave me a *Twilight Zone* vibe. I'd seen the centuries-old show many times while traveling on the ship. Although wearing a helmet, I still felt the need to cover my neck.

How are we supposed to connect with these beings? I thought. And to think, I, Jason Nicholson, was the Communications and Interpretations Officer. Android Thomas stood close behind which gave me more confidence that we could communicate with them.

"Greetings," I said after breaking from the group and kicking up dirt as I headed toward them. My nerves were on high alert, and I was ready to duck, just in case they threw anything. From my experience, I have found some natives to be hostile.

They continued to stare. Not even one blink was released from their huge eyes. They looked as if they could look deep into our souls. Or perhaps, see each heartbeat, every pulse of blood through our arteries and veins. That was the moment I joined Yolonda in the freakout club.

I tossed the fears and thought about other things. The tall individual reminded me of the Maasai people of Kenya back on planet Earth. Although of various builds and heights, these beings all had huge eyes that were out of proportion to their faces compared to most bipeds I have seen. They reciprocated my inquiry, surveying me from the tips of my shoes to the top of my helmet.

"We've come in peace," Android Thomas said as he stepped next to me. "Nosotros Venimos en paz. Venimus in pace."

Still, we got no reply. They did not even blink.

How can Thomas determine their language, if they don't speak, I thought.

Their silence led the android to try other languages, starting with ancient Sumerian. It was very tiring standing and listening to the AI as he spoke the first twenty of over thirty-one thousand Earthly languages.

It did not take long for us to realize the effects of the sun's rising. The ensuing heat forced us to take off our helmets despite the clouds blocking the sun's light. That is when I noticed that the carpels on the plants had softened. Was that movement on the plants that I saw? Perhaps I was hallucinating.

"Let's return to the ship," I said. As Thomas spoke, we turned and moved back to our transport.

"Please excuse their rudeness," I heard the android say as we entered through the ship's door and headed to Decontamination Chambers One and Two.

Leo Zang and I removed our suits and underclothes and entered stalls in Decontamination Chamber One.

"What is that red spot on your neck?" Zhang asked.

I looked in the mirror at my neck. It started to itch.

The shower sprayed hot Straline, a substance that kills most organisms, which did nothing to stop the itching. Next, we were bathed in ultraviolet light. Finally, we received the sauna treatment. The end of decontamination featured lying on tables in the sCAT and mMRI scanners.

Although the exam showed us to be disease-free, the itching increased its volume. I rose from my table, moved to the mirror, and saw a two-centimeter-thick heart-shaped nodule on my neck. When I touched it, the thing itched. I scratched the lump. The more I scraped, the crazier it got. It got to the point where I wanted to burn the thing off.

Within mirror view, I saw that Zhang had one too. The two of us got into our underpants and headed to Sick Bay next door where we were met by Sanchez, Smith, Ahoka, and Yegorova – all of us dressed in green undergarments.

"I see you have a hickey, too," Chloe Smith said. She looked me up and down, and then moved her glance to my neck.

"What can I say," I responded. The sensations on my neck had quieted a little.

Doctor Shoals, our cyborg physician, and android nurse, Beth, entered the room.

"Please form a line and stand against the wall," Shoals said. I stood between Zhang and Smith.

I watched as the doctor raised a handheld machine to Zhang's neck. The thing released a loud buzz.

"Looks like some type of mosquito bite," Shoals said.

"It feels like it too," Zhang said. I flinched as the doctor jabbed the bite on Zhang's neck with a thick needle.

"They must love you very much," said the doc when he moved to me. I had braced for the needle's impact. It was too late because the nurse had jabbed me before he spoke. I felt a little pain minutes later.

"Alien mosquitoes," I said as Shoals moved on to Smith. The thought hit me that the tiny insects could enter the android because there were small spaces on his body. What such an insect could do to Thomas, I did not know.

The bump started to itch again. It was driving me crazy.

"Don't scratch it!" nurse Betty ordered as she grabbed my arm.

I heard a loud thump. Zhang had fallen to the floor.

Day 2

I awakened lying on a cot in the Contamination room. It was apparent to me that quarantine was my new home. Lifting my head, I looked around the ward. The entire boarding party was in the room except for Android Thomas. I attempted to sit up in bed.

"What! Why am I strapped to this bed?" My struggles were futile. Plus, exhaustion ruled.

Three androids entered the room. I, Jason Nicholson, was not the only one struggling to rise.

"You are anemic," the cyborg doctor with "Doctor Johnson" on his nameplate said. "Plus, while unconscious, you tried to bite me. You were apparently hungry for blood. Like everyone else in this ward."

I was shocked, felt weak, and thirsty. Despite my condition, duty still called. I needed to communicate with G&P.

"Did Android Thomas communicate with the locals?" I asked.

"No," Android nurse Ann answered.

"How long have we been here?" Kateryna Yegorova, who was in the bed next to me, asked. I noticed that her eyes were swollen.

"One day," the nurse answered.

I do not know if it was the shot the doctor gave me or my condition, but one thing was certain: The sandman was pouring tons of sleep on my eyelids.

Upon awakening, the first thing I saw was Android nurse Joan's grey eyes. Her stare was spooking me out.

"They need you in communications," she said.

Looking down at my arms and feet, I noticed that the straps to my arms and legs were gone. A purple film covered my eyes. I blinked several times, and it went away.

"You are good and healthy," the nurse said. "Rise slowly. Take your time."

My clothes were at the head of my bed. I rose, got dressed, and followed the nurse to the exit. While walking, I noticed that everyone else was rising from their beds. One of the patients was Commander Uhura.

"Headquarters needs to talk to you," the nurse said.

I walked down two halls and took three elevators before getting to the communications room.

"Earth Station to Prospector One."

"This is Prospector One," I said over the mic after taking a seat at the aluminum desk.

"G and P wants to speak to you."

"Connect. S G One," I said and waited for the company G&P, known to us crewmembers as Greedy and Proud Corporation, to communicate.

"S G One. Jason Nicholson to Prospector One on Lambda Delta.

"Lambda Delta, Jason Nicholson S G One speaking. One, five, zero, delta, three, epsilon.

"What is going on there?" the voice said over the computer's speaker. I assumed it was AI by the way it spoke. "We've heard something about an infection?"

John Feese, my subordinate, entered the room and gave me five pages of findings. I scoured over the first two pages and then went to the medical results page on the computer. The results said that we suffered from mosquito bites and anemia.

"We were bitten by alien mosquitos," I said. "Sending the results."

"Have you communicated with the natives?"

"No," I responded. "Not as I know of." I looked around the room. No one begged to differ.

The AI responded quickly. "Sending troops to get the Lanthanum. You are in eternal quarantine. We thank you. Your families will be compensated. It will be quick."

I swallowed hard because I knew the message meant the crew was expendable. We had done our best to not get infected. All the protocols were followed. It angered me that we and the natives were worth less than these minerals the company wanted. But we knew that was what they did. G and P did it on Bulgorthia and Widerwine. Like the Romans, no mercy is shown. At least my family back home will be well compensated.

Although I noticed it before, no mind was paid to the fact that my eyes had a strange purple haze in front of them. Was I going blind?

Signing off the computer, I heard a sound.

"How'd they get in here?" I asked when I saw the natives in the room. One of them stood in front of the others. She looked like a female from Earth except for some differences in anatomy. I thought she might be a queen because she had a crownlike object, an elongated insect bite encircling her temples and forehead just above the earlobes. Plus, she emitted a vibe of royalty with her subjects standing a short distance behind her.

Mouth agape, I watched as Feese, Sanchez, and Ahoka drew their guns. I also smelled a strange odor.

Throw them away, a voice said in my mind.

I watched as my three crewmembers tossed their weapons clinking into the trash can.

The woman pointed to each of us with her index finger and then beckoned for us to follow. She turned and headed for the door.

I tried to resist. Couldn't. I had to follow her as did the others.

Welcome to my kingdom world, she said in my mind.

***

The ships are within firing range. The queen has us heading for the caves. I figure she controls us with pheromones. I don't mind. It looks like I will get to live. Life here is not bad. We each have been given a role in this kingdom. The food and vision are great, and everyone is satisfied. I don't think I'll miss Earth.

The queen has given us much understanding of her history. They have been invaded before by even more powerful beings than we Earthlings. I have met them, too. I have learned that the Corporation's forces will bombard this planet until there is no resistance. Then, they will have their bots mine the Lanthanum in the mountains while the cyborg and android soldiers stand guard over their treasures. The mosquitos will infiltrate the soldiers, bots, and machines and then travel back to the corporation and its Earth colonies.

I have also learned a bit about the history of this planet and how these beings began to be. The queen has placed visions in our minds. I see chromosomes and their mutations. Then come scenes of animals and an early scene in Lamia's history.

A huge blanket of red moves over the rocks. *The Solenopsis'* destination is the colony of black ants. As a young boy on Earth, I would have enjoyed seeing the fire ants fighting the black ants. The spectacle of thousands of ants at war was greater than any video game. But this is the new way of the universe. Be they invaders or defenders, the results will now be the same.

It started with a meteorite that landed in a forest. A substance from the meteor landed on the surrounding plants which mutated as a result. The sunflower-like plants grew and drew the mosquitos to their blue gemlike carpels. The tiny insects found a home in the carpels. At night and on cloudy days the little vampires sought blood. The first major victim was an ant colony near the plants. The mosquitoes invaded and the ants got infected.

Years later, thousands of enemy ants invaded the infected colony. They took the plague back to their colony. The invaders were now one with the invaded, thanks to the body-snatching virus. Eventually, the virus passed from species to species and all animals truly became one with nature thanks to the mosquitoes.

We are vampires in a sense. Our food is a pleasant nectar the plants make from the blood of dying insects and other animals. It is funny how my vision has changed. Everyone looks like a cartoon. My puffed eyes can now observe the neurons firing in your brain and I can see your heart beating.

I still have not learned how there began to be one queen.

The earth shakes from the explosions as we sit in one building these marvelous people have made. The underground cities are earthquake-proof.

The queen struts among us. I can feel her pleasure from our arriving on this rock and giving her a chance to spread her babies to other earthlike planets. The explosions are the drumbeats of war, and the corporation and Earth colonies have no clue about their fates.

***

My family arrives later today. I am in Heaven right now because besides seeing them, I am also at Yolanda Sanchez's funeral. She died in a freak accident.

We sit around the small knoll containing her corpse. On top of the mound are the flowers draining her body of blood, some of which we drink. I position my mouth under the plant and squeeze a petal. The nectar containing bits of Yolanda's blood is sweet manna. I get a feeling it contains a psychedelic substance because I sense that she is near. It's like she is right beside me laughing and joking.

She has become one with nature and I see what she sees. This moment reminds me of two ADEs, or Asymptotic Demise Experiences, that I witnessed others having. Ages ago they were called Near Death Experiences. At that time, I did not believe in religion nor that science mumbo jumbo saying our bodies give us pleasant experiences at death. The first ADE incident shocked me when Dak Jones had one on the *Prime One* craft as we traveled to Bulgorthia. The other incident happened to a Kaschnittker biped on Primus Nine. Both had died, traveled to unearthly places, and told me things I did that they could not have possibly seen while unconscious. That such distinct beings would have similar experiences was morbid to me.

As if attached to her skin, I see myself flying with Yolanda through a dark tunnel and into the awesome rainbow-colored light. I feel like the universe or some higher being cares about me. Yolanda loves me and she knows the feeling is mutual. We fly over a field of plants that flash like lightning bugs. Viewing them reminds me of the stars, nebulas, and galaxies I have seen on my travels.

There is an interruption in our bond. I have a vision of the silver ship bearing my family. It is flying toward the spaceport that circles this moon. My wife Marnaercious, and my children Ja and Sallyria gaze from the spaceship down at our rock. The beams from their smiles and their delight enthrall me.

I say "bye" to Yolanda as she moves into what looks like a supernova. She responds that she will see us soon.

As tears trickle down my face, I rise from the grass.

"I'll see you guys later," I say to the other mourners.

Still clothed in bliss, I run to the hovdisk and climb aboard. My destination is Dash Airport where I will finally meet my family.

Dash is how I arrived on Titan. This airport was the second site the robots and androids had built after building the spaceport. I helped terraform this moon. I was given some land and sent for my family, who are bringing the money G&P had given them before the company fell under the queen's power.

I am amazed at how well the queen communicates with her subjects so far away from the kingdom fifty light years radial distance. As I understand it, the virus only took two years to conquer Earth and its colonies. Her kingdom spans three-hundred- fourteen light years circumference in all directions.

"Dad," Sallyria says as she runs on the concourse towards me with her arms held wide open. The bliss covers me from the souls of my feet to the curls on my head. No one could have written a better script.

A Good Meal
Guy Belleranti

the
crew
exits
their spacecraft
eager to explore
the planet for alien life
and soon meets a terrestrial tentacled creature
with a smile on each tentacle
and are surprised when
the creature
invites
them
to
dinner
however
the meal goes awry
when the smiling tentacles stop
smiling and begin scowling and snorting and sneering
and the crew wish they were elsewhere
when the tentacles
pull them close
and suck
them
dry

Goody Gumdrop
Stephen McQuiggan

Stan could hear his wife nattering away out in the hall. He turned the telly up to drown out her chatter and gave his groin a furtive scratch. Who the hell was calling at this time of night anyway? Surely it could have waited until morning.

He heard the front door close and breathed a sigh of frustrated relief; perhaps now he'd get the cup of tea he'd been promised and he'd be able to settle down and watch the end of the movie in peace.

"Who was it?" he called out as he heard the click of his wife's heels in the hallway.

Elsa poked her head through the door, a broad smile on her face. "It was Lizzy Knock from next door."

Stan felt his gut rumble and sour at the mere mention of their neighbour. "And what did *she* want?"

Elsa's smile grew ever wider. "She won a bottle of champagne in some raffle or other – proper stuff too, none of your sparkly supermarket wine.'"

"She call round just to boast about that?"

"Of course not," Elsa's eyes were sparkling now too. "Lizzy doesn't drink. She popped round to," with the flourish of a trainee magician, Elsa produced a magnum of champagne from behind her back, presenting it label first to her husband, "see if we might like it. Wasn't that awful good of her? She's always so thoughtful. We could keep it for your birthday at the weekend."

Stan said nothing, swallowing down a retort; he knew Elsa would beat him with it the rest of the night if he dared to utter it. How he *loathed* Lizzy Knock. He wouldn't mind so much if she were a bible thumper, at least there would be some excuse for her showy generosity, or terminally ill or something, but unfortunately she wasn't. He had nothing to rail against except her charity, and doing that made him seem petty and small. It would also lead to him having to make his own cup of tea.

Damn you Lizzy, little Miss Goody Gumdrop, how I'd love to take that champagne bottle and insert it right up your generous –

"Oh," said Elsa, "I happened to mention to her that you were heading into the city tomorrow and she said she's going in too. She's offered to drive you, so make sure you're ready by ten. Wasn't that sweet of her?"

Stan grimaced as a fountain of acid sprayed the wall of his gut; it felt anything but sweet.

"I'll just pop this in the fridge," Elsa held the bottle up like an F1 winner, "and stick the kettle on."

Stan broke into a sweat as he tried to formulate an escape plan, his nerves only settling when he hit upon the idea of a fake phone call from his boss, informing him the conference in the city was to be held at a much earlier hour.

"I'll have to get the first train instead," he practiced as his wife rummaged through the kitchen cupboards, undoubtedly looking for the last of the éclairs which Stan had already ate. Pleased with the bulletproof nature of his excuse he felt his heart rate return to normal.

Why, exactly, did his neighbour's random, unasked for acts of kindness bother him so damn much? Stan was at a loss to say – he felt deep down, on some kind of cellular level, that Lizzy Knock was *wrong* somehow, that her goodwill was slowly sucking the life out of him. Just because you liked children that didn't make you a good person. The nicer she was the more repulsed he became. Yet, because everyone else thought she'd a homemade halo and a harp, he had to bottle his misgivings up until they festered in him and grew septic, gnawing at him from the inside out.

No-one was that nice. She ran on a vanity battery, charged by compliments. She was obviously playing a game. Every little gift, every word of encouragement or pat, uplifting axiom, made him miserable. Her concern was, in itself, concerning.

That weekend, his birthday weekend no less, Stan arrived home slightly late knowing that all the guests would already be there and that the party would be ready to swing: It was his thirty-ninth – his fortieth would have necessitated a surprise, more guests, and a whole lot more palaver. It was going to be a nightmare, but all that could wait for another year. Tonight was going to be perfect he told himself, as he let himself in.

Most of his old mates would be here, and Elsa's brother, Jake, who they usually only saw at Christmas. He had no work in the morning – a night of laughter and carefree indulgence lay ahead. Stan's smile fell from his face as he followed the sound of Nineties grunge and tipsy tittering out into the back garden – the first person he clapped eyes on, backlit by the setting sun, was old Goody Gumdrop Lizzy Knock herself – queen of the weak tea women, whoring for praise as usual.

She was wearing a party hat (how she managed to fit it over her crown of thorns was anybody's guess) and leading an out of tune and raucous *For He's a Jolly Good Fellow*. Whenever Stan had downed his first beer, shaken hands with all and sundry, and had his back slapped so many times he thought a lung might pop out of his mouth, he managed to corner his wife in the kitchen.

"What the hell is *she* doing here?" He didn't try to hide his contempt. It was his birthday; he was entitled to be angry.

"Who?"

"Lizzy bloody Knock!"

Elsa's face tightened. "Oh, Stanley, don't be like that. I've spent all day getting everything ready and –"

"I'm sorry, love," Stan butted in, eager to ward off the waterworks. "Everything's lovely, it really is. You've done a helluva job, truly. I just wondered why you'd invite *her* – it was supposed to be close family and friends, that's all."

"I didn't invite her as such," Elsa said. "She popped round with a cake she'd baked for you. I couldn't very well turn her away after that, could I? Besides," she pointed over to a humungous cake, slathered in baby blue icing, on the table, "look at the trouble she's gone to. It was really awfully nice of her to –"

"Okay, okay," Stan knew when he was beaten. He would just avoid Lizzy and get royally drunk, but he wouldn't touch her damn cake; not a slice, not a solitary crumb.

Although he sometimes caught a glimpse of her in the corner of his eye, and though she insisted on helping Elsa with the washing up, and although she roped all the women into playing interminable, ridiculous party games, Stan managed to hold his tongue and have a good night regardless.

She knew how to work her mojo; he'd give her that. It was all some form of perception deception. She was a walking green screen; anything could be projected onto her.

He was up early next morning, parched and paranoid as usual after a night's drinking, having a smoke in the back garden when his bleary eyes alighted on the half-eaten cake. It really was enormous, encased in a dandruff storm of hundreds and thousands – I'll be forced to eat that for the next month, he thought, and each and every time it would be served up with a hefty helping of the ode of St Lizzy and her benevolent ways.

Fuck that, thought Stan, putting his cigarette out on the squidgy blue icing. He lifted the cake by its flashy silver tray and carried it down to the bottom of the lawn, balancing it on the fence whilst he jiggled open the gate and lifted the lid on the bin. The cake made a satisfying slap as it hit the bottom, the bin rocking slightly on its wheels.

"I take it you didn't enjoy my rainbow gateau then?"

Stan's flesh prickled; he cursed himself for not checking the coast was clear. He turned around to find Lizzy (*Knock, Knock – Who's there? – Lizzy fucking Knock, she always is*) directly behind him.

"Oh, hello," he said in the sort of cheery voice only attainable to those caught red-handed in the midst of a shameful act. "Did you enjoy yourself at the party last night?"

Stan's mind was racing, searching for plausible excuses – he was diabetic; birds had shit on it; it was too nice, he'd eat it all in one go and get fat – rejecting each in turn. Not that it mattered – Lizzy wasn't in the mood for pleasantries.

"I spent hours baking that. If you didn't like you could have returned it. I could have left it down to the hospice; at least they would have appreciated it."

Stan stammered out a few conciliatory grunts before (in keeping with all those caught red-handed) eventually giving way to a surge of self-righteous anger.

"No-one asked for a damn cake in the first place!" He thought himself intimidating until he remembered he was wearing a onesie. He wiped the sludge of cream and sugar from his hands and turned back to the gate, already formulating a version of events that he could relate to Elsa, a version in which Lizzy was the undoubted villain.

"I know you don't like me." Lizzy didn't sound petulant or whiny, merely curious. 'Why is that, do you think? I mean, everyone else does. I help out the whole neighbourhood, volunteer on every committee, babysit half the kids for a two mile radius, organise –'

"That's just it," Stan felt giddy – now was the long dreamed of moment when he got to tell Goody Gumdrop exactly what he thought of her, right to her pious face, "you do far too much."

Lizzy laughed. This wasn't how she reacted in the oft played scenarios Stan was fond of concocting.

"I make you feel inferior," she said, folding her arms like a schoolmarm. "I hold up a mirror to your own selfish inadequacies and you cannot bear to look."

"No," Stan flushed. There *was* a smidgeon of truth in what she said, but he would clamber into the bin and eat her rancid cake before he ever admitted that to her, or himself. "People like you, the little Dolly Do-Gooders, are all hiding something. You're all trying to atone for something; all your deeds are a distraction, a disguise. I wouldn't trust you as far as I could spit."

Lizzy's face stretched into a grin. Stan was appalled at the change it lent her – her bland, washed-out housewife demeanour now replaced by the visage of a feral, and quite possibly rabid, dog.

Did her eyes just turn completely back? I think her eyes just turned completely –

"How very perceptive, Stanley – it's not often I come across those who see through me."

Stan was caught unawares; usually her mouth was a Lazy Susan of insincere compliments, the last thing he expected was for her to agree with him. He wandered back over to her, his face scrunched up in puzzlement as he waited for the punchline. He cursed himself for not bringing his phone so that he could record her confession and play it to Elsa, to everyone, next time they sang Goody's praises. "You admit it's all an act then?"

"Oh, it's certainly not selfless but it's no act. I do it to live, Stanley. Peoples' gratitude is meat and drink to me."

"Spare me the happy-clappy bible bullshit. I thought even you were above all that."

"Oh no," Lizzy said, unbuttoning her blouse, "I mean it quite literally."

Stan's guts rolled and flopped in much the same squelchy manner the cake had slid off the tray and into the bin. Lizzy's bare chest was devoid of breasts, of skin – it was nothing more than a huge, toothless, sucking mouth. It pulsed and spasmed obscenely before Lizzy demurely covered herself up once more.

Stan fell back against the garden fence, his hands feebly swatting before him. He felt as if he were wading through a clogged sewer. "Stay away from me," he croaked. His chest had tightened to an alarming degree and he wondered if this was how it all ended.

"Me? You know I'm only trying to help."

Lizzy leant over him; there was a rancid stench emanating from her, sharp beneath the perfume. Stan tasted it in the back of his throat as his heavy legs tried desperately to function in unison.

"'I know what you're thinking," she said, her lips non-existent in that wolfish grin, "you think you're going to run inside and tell your dinky little wife all about me, then call the police. Good luck with that."

There was no laughter in her eyes now; there was nothing there at all.

"I'm head of the Women's Union and I run an outreach program for cancer kids. I raise thousands for charity every year. Next week I'm running a marathon for Spina Bifida – did you know Inspector Murray's daughter suffers from that very affliction? I'm sure he'll mobilise the entire force whenever you inform him I'm some sort of monster."

"That's exactly what you are! You're a . . ." all Stan could think of was the sucking maw hidden away beneath the flimsiest of fabrics, ". . . a vampire!"

Lizzy appeared to consider this for a moment. "A vulgar term for such a unique being as myself, don't you think? I feed on gratitude, not blood." She smoothed down her skirt and sighed. "I'll have to consider what to do with you. I'm not ready to move on just yet. I've built up quite the reputation here – it could be years before the inevitable resentment kicks in and I'm forced to find a new feeding ground. But don't worry, I'll think of something – probably on my run next week. I always have my best ideas whilst running. Toodle pip, Stanley."

She leant over and scratched his forehead with her nail; it felt like an icy kiss. She glided away as silently as she had arrived. He waited until she was out of sight before bolting back inside. Elsa was in the kitchen, hugging a mug of tea against her dressing gown.

"What the hell's up with you?" she winced as he slammed the back door. "You look like you've seen a ghost."

"Worse," Stan began, and then realised the truth of Lizzy's mockery. His face scalded with the sudden flush of angry blood.

"Listen to me," he seethed, "you are never to see Lizzy Knock again – never speak to her, never answer the door to her, never so much as look at her." His hands were shaking uncontrollably. "Understand?"

Elsa gave him one of her patented, withering looks. "I suggest you go back to bed and don't surface again until you've sobered up: Understand?"

Stan knew when he was beaten (and he *could* do with a lie down) so he complied without further hostilities breaking out. He would reason with her whenever his nerves had settled down.

Yet, if anything, his wife consorted more than ever with Lizzy. Stan grew weary of putting his foot down (in ever more swampy soil) and took to staying out when Lizzy come calling. It was a tactic designed as much to save his marriage as anything else – his inability to stop griping about his neighbour, to hide the grimace when her very name was mentioned, to stop from screaming that same name when he awoke bathed in sweat from his increasingly frequent nightmares, was beginning to drive a wedge between him and Elsa.

I didn't really see that awful mouth, he kept telling himself, *I was hungover and delusional. She's nothing more than a do-gooding busybody that I let get to me.* But still the night terrors gripped him, seeped into his waking life.

He learned to hide his feelings (though nothing could eradicate the twitch of his eye when in the proximity of her) but it became ever more difficult as the weeks rolled by. *I'm playing the long game,* he assured himself, *I'm Edmond fucking Dantes.*

Lizzy had stepped up her campaign of altruism to a level that had the entire town buzzing. Step into any shop and you were bound to be regaled with tales of her latest exploits before you managed to hook out the change for the paper – not that Stan bought the local rag now; Lizzy had become a regular feature, appearing on the front page as often as not with some sickly waif or other.

The newsprint seemed to corrode his skin. As he gazed into those oh-so- kindly eyes, all he could hear was the squelch of that hungry, sucking mouth. With every awestruck report Stan felt the spot on his forehead, where Lizzy had scraped her nail, throb dully as a hoar frost penetrated his skull, numbing his neurons and leaving him lost and anxious, unaware of who or what he was.

Elsa began working on all of Lizzy's projects and was rarely home until Stan was in bed – a threefold blessing that Stan was grateful for, because (1) It meant Lizzy was not in his house so much; he had become frightened of her presence to a degree that shamed him. He once burst into tears when she offered up a simple "hello"; (2) With all her new found zeal for charity, Elsa was bright-eyed and upbeat and less prone to dwell on his faults. In the short time they now spent together they got on better than ever. And, best of all, (3) Elsa had taken to leaving him casseroles and stews to heat up for himself when he got home from work, each one more delicious than the last.

Elsa's crusade to help the helpless had certainly improved her culinary skills and he was thankful her goodwill also extended to him. Stan, although anxiety fed greedily on his insides, even managed to put on weight. Things were far from perfect, but at least the new routine he found himself enmeshed in allowed Stan some much needed peace of mind.

But contentment is a fickle, temporary thing as Stan found out when, seated at his desk crunching out numbers on his laptop, he heard a couple of the office temps say that Elizabeth Knock (*'Y'know, she's like Mother Teresa only with better hair*) had been nominated for the local Citizen Award.

A bolt of ice stabbed Stan's forehead, shattering his synapses and throwing him from his seat, his coffee pooling in his lap; a detail he was to be thankful for later when he'd realised he'd pissed himself.

When he managed to extract himself from the sympathetic scrum that surrounded him, assuring his co-workers he was fine and that he definitely didn't need to go to the hospital, Harrigan, the manager, told him to take a few days off and "recharge the old batteries." Stan was only too willing to accept; he did seem to be running on empty lately.

When Elsa got home and he told her the travails of the day (but not what had triggered them) she declared she was clearing her calendar to nurse him back to health. She waved away his protests with a stern shake of her head.

"You look like death warmed up, Stanley. You're the colour of watered- down milk. I've been worried about you for weeks now. It's high time we nipped this in the bud and got you back on your feet. You're not getting out of that bed again until I see a glow back in those cheeks, okay?"

Stan assented, happy that his wife cared so much and that he had nothing to do, and all the time in the world to do it in. Yet as the days slipped slowly by, the hours accumulating like the crumbs between his sheets, Stan grew more sickly. He found it hard to differentiate between his waking state and the fevered delirium that plagued his dreams. His body would spasm and he found it difficult to co-ordinate his thoughts with his speech. It was all he could do to stop his wife from calling in a doctor.

By the fourth day, his bed had become a sodden prison and he could no longer stomach the food that Elsa brought him. It smelt delicious, it tasted great, but once he had swallowed a spoonful his gut would rebel.

"'m sorry," he said, as Elsa chewed on her lip and lifted the dish away, "you're cooking's wonderful, I just can't . . ."

She sat down on the bed beside him and smiled ruefully. "You know my cooking's awful. I could never so much as boil an egg. I thought you would've twigged on sooner to be honest."

"Twigged on to what?"

"Lizzy's been cooking for you, helping me out since I've been volunteering. The woman's a marvel. Honestly, I don't know where she finds the time to –"

Stan began to convulse violently. He could see Elsa leaning over him, trying to hold him down, and then she faded and all he could see was a mouth – a huge, toothless sphincter – pulsing, throbbing, *sucking*.

In a rare moment of lucidity Stan opened his eyes and took in his surroundings. Everything was so white. It was as if the whole world had been erased leaving only a vase of flowers, a too bright fluorescent tube, and a highly uncomfortable bed.

Where am I? He thought; his tongue too swollen to produce anything more subtle than a muffled groan. A face loomed over him, coming slowly into focus. Stan's heart began to sprint from a standing start – he tried to raise his arms to push that wolfish face away but they were strapped to his sides.

"We're awake today I see," Lizzy beamed. "That makes a pleasant change."

Stan spat out a stream of garbled invective but, whether Miss Knock understood or not, it did not alter her sweet demeanour one jot.

"Easy tiger," she cooed, "you'll do yourself a mischief, though there's lots of nurses about to help you if you do."

Stan's eyes rolled around the room, searching, pleading.

"You're on the Psych Ward, Stanley. You've had yourself a breakdown, you silly boy. I guess I *am* partly to blame." Lizzy leaned over him; Stan could feel the unseen mouth pressing against his chest. "They do say you can kill with kindness."

Stan screamed, the bed rocking as he put the last of his energy into trying to flee from the creature perched above him. Two nurses came running, though in his frantic mind they were little more than vague blurs.

"The branch is creaking, Stanley; how long will you be able to hang on?" Lizzy whispered. "I'll have to go and help poor Elsa clear the drive – never turn a hearse in it the state it's in at present."

"I think you'd best leave now, Miss Knock," one said, whilst the other produced a needle. A warm calm followed the jag and Stan stopped his writhing.

"Was that his wife?" he heard one of the blurs ask as he drifted down into the silent abyss.

"No, that's Lizzy Knock – y'know, the Citizen of the Year. She visits him every day. She really is nothing short of an angel."

Me That Was
Tyree Campbell

No friends, only competitors
No sunrises

Romantic walks at night in the park
do not end well

Nightly drudgery
over and over,
forever

I could . . .
or I could . . .
But no matter what I do
the song, as they say,
remains the same

I stare for hours at a faded photograph
Mom and Dad, Billy & me . . .
. . . *sigh*

Necking
Christopher Ananias

Scores sat in the cool back row watching the late show at the Diana Theatre. A sinister French film pounded out of the enormous side speakers, but he lost interest in reading the subtitles.

Instead, he watched people's heads and slices of their hairy faces, bald faces, caked with makeup faces, faces licking other faces, faces glared up in their phones like long-nosed Jack-o'-lanterns. Faces with hopes and dreams, one face, his haughty face—he was sure—had no soul.

People moved around, playing musical chairs, going to the restroom, or concessions for Mike's assorted candies, Cokes, and popcorn tubs. Then his eye fell on the white neck of a clean-shaven man who held Scores's interest the entire time. Like some kind of Modigliani painting of a long neck coming out of the dark.

Scores saw the man with the beautiful white neck flying past the usher. Gone. Scores stepped onto the sidewalk feeling like he'd lost something special. His shadow stretched before him like a monster in the moonlight.

Scores thought the movie had a surreal quality, and that's how the night seemed . . . like he was the leading character in a sinister French film, but he couldn't speak French.

He regretted not trying to understand it, because there was a brutal scene that drew his full attention. Then he gave up again when their flowery spitting dialogue drew out into paragraphs of subtitles to read.

Scores walked up to his darling Mini Cooper, popped the hood, and waited. The cars hurried out, brake lights flashing, and gunning motors. It surprised him no one came to his aid. He thought more about the French movie. A movie board whacked down inside his head. Act II The Stranded Motorist Scene.

Scores kept the faith, he knew someone would try to help or hurt him eventually in the deserted parking lot. The orange sodium arc lights made him look weird, like he had jaundice. Even his beloved red-and-white stripped Mini Cooper looked a sickly orange in the sulfur glow.

Headlights swooped across the parking lot. He psyched himself up for the nocturnal encounter. You could never be too careful around the night people.

Act III The Ruse. The movie board clacked!

"You need a jump, bud?" said a big oval face from an idling Ford Bronco.

"I'm out of gas can you believe that?" said Scores with a sad "What am I going to do?" smile that looked rather pretty in his teenie-bopper pink T-shirt. He was a pretty man.

"You need a ride to the gas station, I've got a can," said the large man, thinking unlike his hetero self, *that's a hot man.*

"That would be great. Let's go!" Scores opened the passenger door and slammed it.

"Easy dude." The man frowned and reluctantly said "I'm Bob. What's your name?"

Scores laughed and said, "I'm sorry. I-I saw this movie and-and . . ." Then he started laughing.

The man's face relaxed and his thick lips turned upward, exposing a broken tooth, and he chuckled a little. "What was it about?"

"Ok-ok," Scores got himself under control, "I'm not sure. I couldn't understand it . . . But this big French guy tore an old lady's purse off her shoulder and jerked her into the gravel. Really hurt her—knees and elbows all bloody. Screaming! He took off with it on his shoulder like a big fat ass model walking the runway." Then another laughing fit.

"Geez, mister what's so funny about that?"

"I don't know. I'm kind of sick." Scores eyebrows went down and his bottom lip stuck out.

Bob thought, *hum.* Looking at how delicate Score's looked with his small hands and thin white arms in the tight pink shirt. *I shouldn't be attracted to him, but he's gorgeous and nuts.* "Well, are you on medication?"

"Sometimes, but not for a while. Has anyone ever told you, you have a nice neck?" said Scores, smiling titling his head, looking ever so pretty to Bob.

"What?"

"I want to give you a hickey."

Bob studied Scores, and there was something about his full lips, glossed with red lipstick. How his dark long hair was curled up at the end on his shoulder, and the way it framed his high cheekbones. His thin little waist. He was a very petite man.

Bob put the truck back into park. "Maybe you could start on my neck and see where it goes?"

"Sure. Okay just sit still."

Act IV The Final Scene of Scores French movie. Clack!

Scores climbed onto Bob, coming in like a lover. He kissed and licked on his throat, tasting sweaty salt and a bitter cologne. Bob jerked at the first nibble, and whiskers bristled under Score's lips. His tongue and teeth searched for a thumping artery in the layers of fat and moles. Scores thought about the other man's smooth white neck, that he watched in the theatre, imagining a beautiful blue throbbing artery. Bob closed his eyes and drifted off into some warm pleasant place. The full blackness of night came curling down as the moon disappeared in the dark clouds, and the rain beaded down the windshield.

Phantoms
Eddie Spohn

The distress beacon came on suddenly, a pattern of chirps against the background hiss of the cosmos. Someone nearby was in trouble and reaching out for help. A situation that should not be.

Upon hearing it, Sandra Mirandez glanced across the bank of controls at her nearest companion, a navigator/co-pilot named Gene Brigg. Brigg was looking down at a screen displaying rows of code, giving the final human sign-off on the computer's plotting for their course home. The crew of their ship, *Flaming Telepath*, was just about to go into the freezers for the three- year trip home to Ersatz 5. He heard the rhythmic chirps and looked up to roll his eyes. "Who the hell would be out here?" he wondered aloud.

"I don't know," Sandra said, running a scan of the immediate sector. The origin point of the distress signal was a small dot just coming out of the daylight side of Gitrew, the planet whose night side disc filled most of the view outside the ship's windows. Way up along one blue-edged horizon was a pinprick of yellow light, visible on Sandra's scanner but not yet to the naked eye. "The tags aren't in the database," Sandra said.

"Why does that not surprise me?" Brigg muttered. "Probably a bunch of scrappers who got blown off course."

"Just what we need," Sandra said.

There was a brisk resale trade of harvested space junk. Some of the scrappers did not limit it to refuse and stole items still in use, such as satellites and mining equipment. A ship like the one issuing the beacon, this far out, was certainly suspicious.

"Maybe we can pretend we didn't hear them?" Brigg said, only half joking.

"Sure, so when they die we have a party of marshals waiting to arrest us when we land." Sandra told him. "There's a record of the beacon in the computer now, so unless we want to be spending our bonuses on lawyers' fees we better check it out."

Brigg cleared his throat. "I bet the company would thank us for saving on the trouble and expense of bringing them back home with us."

"Secretly, *probably,*" Sandra said with a smirk. "*Officially?* They would be right there with the lawyers putting us on the fire for ignoring GP."

GP stood for Galactic Protocol, the code that all travelers (law abiding ones) in the void were compelled to follow. Its main tenet was that aid was to be rendered to any ship in distress, regardless of its world of origin or mission, and crew were to be taken to the first civilized world.

"Dammit," Brigg said and got on the loudspeaker to inform the *Flaming Telepath*'s own crew that their impending sleep was about to be delayed. He could not actually hear it, but he imagined their groans of protest echoing through the corridors.

Sandra attempted contact with the craft. "This is the Huros Company mining vessel *Flaming Telepath,* out of Ersatz 5, speaking to unidentified vessel in distress. Are you receiving? Over." She oscillated through the radio bandwidths but received no answer other than the repetitive chirps of the distress beacon. This meant the normal transmitter could be down, or . . .

"Maybe the crew's dead," Brigg said, plucking the thought from her head.

That was something that had to be determined. The only way to do *that* was to intercept the craft. By now other crew members were coming up to the flight deck to see what was going on. Pneumatic doors whooshed to allow a crowd of agitated people into an instrument filled room designed for the comfort of five of them. The group made way for Captain Crowley and First Mate Jermil, who plopped down in their normal seats. Yeagorian, the pilot, settled into the last proper seat in the row, while the rest of the crew looked on over their heads at the bank of screens and winking displays.

Captain Crowley shook his head. "I leave you two up here alone for a few minutes and look what happens."

Sandra appeared hurt. "They came over the terminator from Gitrew's dayside."

The captain pondered this. "Huros has full rights to this place. It's bought and paid for. We were down there for two years and we never saw anything orbiting. *Now* they show up?"

It was a rhetorical question that no one attempted to answer. Yeagorian's intercept of the craft was fully plotted, and she looked to the captain for the order to initiate. Her co-pilot and navigator Brigg was at her side. Captain Crowley gave them the nod and Yeagorian pressed a button at the end of a toggle switch. *Flaming Telepath* shivered with a momentary rumble as the thrusters blinked enough to overcome inertia, and began moving imperceptibly to the humans on board, but with great actual speed in the direction of the other ship. Within minutes, the ship was no longer detectible only on Sandra's view-screen as a point of light, but could be seen through the flight deck's windows. It grew from a speck of illumination to a broken up line of them, the running lights outlining the smooth hull structure of a light cruiser.

"Well they aren't scrappers, at least," Brigg said when he saw the ship, secretly glad they would not have to deal with that brand of often smelly riff-raff.

Crowley looked to the line of faces peering over the backs of the flight deck seats. "Shuttle detail," he said and picked four of the gathering. "Brigg, you do the flying." There were moans from those among the chosen who were miners rotating back to Ersatz; after surviving their five-year shifts in the mines, the last thing they wanted to do was risk themselves on a rescue mission. But as fellow travelers of the void, they understood the precarious nature of being a human floating in the proverbial tin can, and that someday they themselves might require assistance.

"And bring arms," Crowley told them. "Just in case."

This brought a glint into the eyes of a couple of the shuttle crew, turning their frowns upside down.

Reverse thrusters flashed and brought *Flaming Telepath* to a halt less than a mile from the cruiser. The away crew boarded the shuttle, with Brigg as grumbling pilot. He'd been all set to kick back with a nice drink before the big sleep, and then Sandra has to find a distress beacon and ruin everything.

When all was ready, two rectangular sections of *Flaming Telepath*'s hull slid away and the shuttle emerged, clasped at intervals by a trio of extendable metal claws, like a metallic prey item in the grip of a mechanized raptor. A countdown began, and when it reached zero, the metal claws opened and retracted back into *Flaming Telepath*, the plates on the hull sliding shut again.

The shuttle was now an independent entity, connected to the mothership by radio alone. "See you in a while, crocodile," Brigg said, unable to see it but knowing Sandra was smiling at her seat in *Flaming Telepath*'s flight deck. He turned the shuttle and crossed the void to the distressed cruiser, a ninety-meter-long arrowhead-shaped vessel, dark except for the running lights and a single lit portal.

Brigg did a brief circle of the craft, scanning the hull with spotlights, each fierce as a sun, and found no exterior damage. "No ID tags or numbers," he reported back to Sandra on *Flaming Telepath*. "Talk about antiques," he said with a whistle. "This baby is old."

The cruiser was not spinning wildly, so he drew up close to it, matching its speed and orbit, lining one of the shuttle's boarding airlocks with one of those on the cruiser and extending the gangplank, which emerged from the shuttle like a ribbed umbilical to connect the two craft. Then he filled the umbilical with pressurized air and the readings indicated the connection was sound.

"Time to say 'hi' to our new friends," Brigg said. "Whoever they are."

The boarding team unbuckled themselves from the row of seats behind Brigg.

"Easy for you to say," said Rea, one of the miners on her way home to Ersatz. "You get to stay behind with the shuttle."

Brigg shrugged with arrogant innocence. "The perks of being a pilot. Flight school is open to everyone. A little bit of studying and you could have been sitting here."

Rea flashed him a not entirely good-natured middle finger and the rest of the team whispered obscenities at him.

"Remember who's flying you back," Brigg reminded them.

The boarding team donned their EP suits, checking and then re-checking the seals. When this was done, they passed through two sets of airlock doors, which opened and closed in succession, and into the umbilical. They crossed this to the cruiser. Rea slid an access panel aside to reveal a flat touchpad beneath a dark oval screen. She took in a sharp breath upon seeing the archaic hardware. "Wow," she said, "I have to say this is a first for me." She typed in a command and the screen lit up with a green glow and rows of information.

"Well she's airtight, anyway," Rea said over her microphone to the others. "No breaches and holding pressure." She pressed the ACCESS button and the doors slid open to an inner room with dim flickering lights. They stepped inside and the outer doors closed on the umbilical. A press of a button and the inner doors slid open, allowing them into a dark corridor. The team switched on the fog lights atop their helmets while Rea messed with the keypad at the nearest bulkhead in an attempt to get some of the cruiser's interior lights on. It was as simple as pressing a single button labelled ENERGIZE.

When the ship lit up, Rea offered an explanation. "Guess they shut everything down to conserve energy."

They made their way down the corridor, searching all of the connecting rooms. So close to the airlock these were only maintenance areas, which revealed nothing but empty interface tables with inert screens surrounded by walls of exposed cable like rubber coated tentacles.

"So that's how they used to do it," someone quipped.

Further on, the corridor crossed a wider hall that bisected the length of the cruiser, from the rear engine pods to the front living quarters. At this point, the boarding team divided up. Two members headed to the rear of the ship. Rea and another miner named Georgi went to the front, slowly making their way through personal quarters, a recreation area, and a cafeteria with plates of decomposing food at some of the tables. At each stop, both teams found areas that had been manually shut down. There had not been a catastrophe, but clearly *something* had happened.

And a *long* time ago.

***

Back on the *Flaming Telepath,* the crew returned to their rooms or entertained themselves in the game rooms while waiting to find out how long it would be before they embarked on the voyage home. The sooner the shuttle returned, the quicker they could all get there. Although once entered, their return trip sleep would be three years, it would subjectively pass the same as any other night's rest.

Sandra Mirandez busied herself on the flight deck going through the rolls of lost spacecraft in the database. The lack of traceable tags and registrations bothered her. So did the ship's apparent age. Brigg's emphatic description of the craft as "really old," was of no help whatsoever.

A nearby speaker emitted the random chatter of the boarding team. At the moment, they were still exploring as-yet empty spaces upon the cruiser. This was punctuated by Brigg's attempts to engage Sandra in inane conversation to pass the time. She was busy on her quest to ID the cruiser and was ignoring him.

Captain Crowley came in with a glass of neurotoxins in one hand. By his brief swaying, the drink was having an effect.

"Celebrating already?" Sandra enquired.

Crowley raised the glass of red fluid. "Think of it as a last hurrah to ensure interesting dreams. So what are you up to?"

"Just being nosy," Sandra answered. "Trying to ID this ship." She pointed out the window at the cruiser and attached shuttle, visible as a smear of light against the night side disc of Gitrew.

"Bet it's just a scuttle from somewhere that got caught in orbit," Crowley offered. "One of those mysteriously lost insurance claims. Or a bunch of scrappers that got too ambitious."

"Maybe," Sandra said. "But the ship is really old. Did you see that?"

"Didn't look too much into it," Crowley admitted. "Just know we have to investigate any distress signals. No one's found anything onboard so far."

They listened for a while to the running dialogue between the teams which had split up to explore the midline of the cruiser. Brigg was trying to get Sandra to engage in a guess- the-word contest: "What's a seven letter word for Captain Crowley that starts with A and ends in E?"

Crowley engaged the transmitter. "Mister Brigg, need I remind you that your attention needs to be on what you are doing and not playing games? If there is an emergency, you may have to get the crew out of there in a hurry. Not to mention that all of this is being recorded."

"Sorry Sir," Brigg replied in a voice crackling with static. Gitrew's turbulent atmosphere played hell with radio transmissions sometimes.

"This is just like *The Ghost Ship*," Sandra said suddenly.

Crowley giggled. "I was wondering how long it would be before you brought up one of your crazy movies."

"It's not just a movie, Captain. It's based on a legend."

"*Exactly*. A legend. A story that's been told so many times that some people think it's true. People like my otherwise trusty crewmember Mirandez."

"Well, what if it's true?"

"What?" Crowley asked, standing a bit unsteadily even though he was leaning against a reinforcing ridge of wall lining the dome of the flight deck. He smirked. "Yeah, I know. A bunch of phantoms floating around space luring the unwary to their deaths. You believe that bunch of crazy nonsense?" He tilted his head with a mischievous smile. "Do I need to put you in for a psych evaluation?"

"I don't know," Sandra told him. She looked down at a suddenly blinking screen. "I just got a potential hit on our cruiser. This thing went missing two thousand years ago. It didn't show up at first because Ident only checks tags from the last hundred years."

Crowley leaned over to read the information on her screen. "You know the old records are sketchy," he told her. "And you're getting a visual match of a style of craft that was pretty common back then. Damn, hard to believe people put their faith in those junk heaps."

"How many of these things do you think are still drifting around?" she enquired pointedly. Sandra read aloud some info highlighted in red.: "'2685, we took onboard an escape pod jettisoned from unknown craft containing six survivors.' That was the last transmission from that ship, so *something* happened."

Crowley frowned. "We don't know if that *is* the same ship, dear. And if it is, whatever happened, happened a *long* time ago."

***

Out on the cruiser, Rea and her boarding team partner, Georgi, made their way into the final chamber in the ship's fore deck. It was someone's personal quarters. The walls hung with hologram foils of musical artists and actors in immersion films . . . *presumably* . . . the depictions were representative of artistic styles that were *ancient*.

At about the same time as their minds processed this strange disconnect, their eyes dropped to the single bunk and the floor immediately around it. This was where they saw the first of the cruiser's crew. A figure lay on its back in the bunk, arms at its side as if dead. It was clothed in garments long gone out of style, and all the skin not covered by clothing was wrinkled and grey, as if all the moisture had been sucked from it. A nimbus of white hair surrounded its head. Its arms were wrapped protectively around another figure at its side, this one much shorter with its face pressed to the first figure's side. There was the impression of a mother and child. Along the base of the bunk, four more humanoid bodies lay, all of them clothed in strangely styled garments and with the same grey and dehydrated corpse flesh.

"We found crew," Georgi said over his headset.

Rea was down on the floor, running a scanner over the chest of the nearest body. She was certain just by the man's appearance that he was dead, but she wanted to be sure, and was not surprised to find the chest cavity as silent as the space outside the cruiser. "He's gone," she said. The figure below her appeared to be a middle aged human dressed in clothing long ago out of style.

What the hell am I doing here? she thought, and riding the tail of that came a total void in her consciousness; all concept of self or biographical history simply *gone*.

Georgi saw Rea suddenly sit straight up in the midst of her scan of the third body on the floor. The ones she had gone over seemed more filled out now as compared to the others. Their flesh had gone from grey to a translucent pink and was no longer so shriveled.

"Rea?" Georgi said. She did not answer. Her face was shrunken and grey through the faceplate of her EP suit. *Just like those corpses,* Georgi thought frantically, then corrected, *the ones she hasn't touched.*

His hand dropped to the butt of his holstered pistol and rested there in shock as he watched Rea's transformation. Her face was contracting into itself, the flesh pulling closer to her skull like an apple in a dehydrator, her eyes bugging out and the color of hard boiled eggs. She looked at him and opened her mouth as if to say something, but only a gurgle came out before she toppled forward.

Three of the corpses sat up and looked at Georgi with glittering eyes full of hunger.

They were amazingly fast, those three newly rehydrated creatures. Now swollen with Rea's nutritious memories, they lunged upon Georgi, pushing him down toward their famished family who had been lying in stasis for untold years. Absorption required only the briefest touch, and those who had already indulged were careful not to take more life until all had fed. The torpid others were sluggish at first, but warmed by the proximity of lived memories, they reached out to absorb Georgi's life essence.

They fed and woke.

And went on a hunt for the rest of the boarding team.

In the uncertainness of space, one could never be accused of gluttony.

***

Onboard the *Flaming Telepath,* Sandra Mirandez and Captain Crowley listened as the intercom played out the drama of Georgi and Rae discovering the presumably dead crew. There was no climactic ending, only a dull empty static as the rest of the boarding team rushed over to them, and in turn their chatter simply ceased to be.

Sandra exchanged a *told-you-so* glance with Crowley.

The captain shook his head. "They're professionals. You need to stop watching all those conspiracy theory immersion films."

But he looked a little worried himself. He pressed a toggle switch and called out for Brigg.

***

Brigg was so comfortable in the shuttle's pilot seat that he fell asleep for a bit, the chatter of the boarding crew in his ear. He dreamed of Ersatz, of days fishing for bonefish in the shoals. He was there in knee deep water, his lure cast farther out into deeper places, his wife and relatives standing nearby (weird because none of them liked to fish).

He hooked into something and fought hard to bring it in. His wife helped him pull in the last few feet of line. She kneeled in the shallows with the hooked fish pressed against her thighs, ribbons of blood coursing down to her knees.

"It's over," she said to him. "Don't fight it."

"Is it?" Brigg asked.

He came to, his dream dissolving to Captain Crowley's frantic calls from the *Flaming Telepath*. He clumsily leaned forward to answer, nearly spiking his face on the microphone protruding from the control panel. "I'm here, Captain."

"We've lost contact with the boarding crew," Crowley said. "Are you in contact with them?"

Brigg was having a hard time concentrating. He felt as if he'd had a few drinks. But he could hear the stomping feet of the returning team crossing the umbilical. "They're coming back now, Captain," he said. "Maybe the shielding on this old ship messed up their radios."

The team was inside the airlock. The inner doors to the shuttle opened. Brigg got to his feet and approached the airlock to meet the returning boarding party but saw no one familiar. A group of six people stood in the room watching him, dressed in archaic clothes and with hungry expressions on their faces. They appeared human enough, but their milky pink translucent flesh was threaded with bloodless vessels, ice blue and wriggling like snakes over strange inner architectures of bone.

Brigg's urge to run, to hide, to fight, dribbled away, and he stood there helpless as they approached, laid fingers upon his body, and sucked all his memories and experience away.

***

Brigg's last transmission came over the intercom of the *Flaming Telepath*, his mistaken belief that the boarding party had returned. After that, quiet static. Sandra Mirandez and Captain Crowley listened to that horrifying white noise, waiting for something, *anything* else.

A mile away in the void, visible through *Flaming Telepath*'s great flight window, the cruiser's thrusters suddenly flared in brief conical jets of blue, fierce and bright against Gitrew's night side. The craft had not been disabled after all, the distress beacon a clever ruse. The cruiser tore free from the shuttle and its attaching umbilical and whisked out of view, leaving in its wake the jettisoned bodies of Brigg and the rest of the boarding crew, spinning like so much discarded refuse in the void of space

"Oh dear," Crowley said, biting his lower lip.

Blood Journey
By Terrie Leigh Relf & Henry Lewis Sanders

Blood Journey is an intricately constructed tale of love and revenge among the undead. The beheading of the evil Baroness Andora by Count Vasilie sets off a chain of events among the followers of the Church of the Dark Mother that threatens to destroy the vampire community. Relf and Sanders follow the trail of blood and darkness that began long ago and far away as they weave an erotic path through the exotic nights of London, lust, and mayhem to slake the thirst of eve the most avid readers of the Dark Side.

https://www.hiraethsffh.com/product-page/blood-journey

The Wolves of Glastonbury
by Edward Cox & Terrie Leigh Relf

What happens in Glastonbury stays in Glastonbury—even if it means the end of one of humanity's longest alternate lifelines. The hunt is on for Claire and Ethan . . .

https://www.hiraethsffh.com/product-page/wolves-of-glastonbury-by-terrie-leigh-relf-edward-cox

Blood Sampler
By David Lee Summers & Lee Clark Zumpe

Two of the finest minds in the genres have amalgamated their resources and imaginations to come up with some of the gothiest and goofiest vampire flash fiction this side of Bucharest. David Lee Summers, of *Tales of the Talisman* and *Heirs of the New Earth* fame, and Lee Clark Zumpe, mild-mannered reporter for a daily metro-Floridian newspaper, take you on a journey through tales that fit everywhere between Type O positive and Type AB negative. With a kickin' cover by Laura Givens and detailed illustrations by Marge Simon, *Blood Sampler* is a must-read even if you don't care for the suckers.

Type: Anthology – vampire – flash fiction

Ordering Link:

https://www.hiraethsffh.com/product-page/blood-sampler-by-david-lee-summers-lee-clark-zumpe

Two of a Kind
Steve Burford

The young man in the casually expensive suit sat at the hotel restaurant table and gave no indication he knew someone was watching his every move. Reaching into an inside pocket, he withdrew a cigarette case.

"I didn't know that vampires smoked."

A woman had separated herself from the shadows at the edge of the room and was now standing by his table. She was tall, dark, and wearing an ironic half-smile. The man rose to his feet. "I'm sorry?"

As if that had been an invitation, the woman pulled out the table's second chair and sat down. "Thank you." She opened a hand purse. "The cigarette," she said whilst searching. "I'll admit it surprised me. Ah, here we are. Light?" She held out a cigarette lighter.

"Thank you." With a faint smile of his own, the man accepted the proffered lighter. "Beautiful," he said. "Silver?"

"Solid."

"And so highly polished, one can see one's own reflection quite clearly in it."

"So you can," she said, "but then I'd checked that one out earlier."

"Ah." The man lit his cigarette and handed the lighter back. "So, what shall we do next? Are you going to pull a crucifix from somewhere about your person? Spray holy water in my face? Or shall we just order a starter of garlic mushrooms in the hope that I'll collapse foaming onto the table cloth?" He waved his cigarette towards the menu. "I do recommend the mushrooms by the way. Shall we order?"

As if telepathic, a quietly deferential waiter materialised, took their orders then vanished as silently as he had arrived.

"You have me at a disadvantage, Miss . . . ?"

"Yes. I have. And have had for some time." The vampire's brow furrowed very slightly and she laughed, a surprisingly deep sound. "But if you're looking for a name, you can call me . . . Angela, Mr. Weston."

"Please. You are my guest. It seems. And if you know my last name, you must also know my first."

Angela nodded. "Peter," she said, and again there was that half-smile of someone who understood the game of assumed names they were both playing. "Well, Peter, I suppose it would be only polite to tell you that I've come here to kill you."

The vampire nodded again as if this merely confirmed something he already knew. "It does usually happen the other way around, you know. Still, I do hope that you'll wait until after the last course. Ah, the wine."

A second waiter had arrived, and for a few minutes, the vampire played out the ritual of tasting and accepting that such exclusive establishments demanded of their guests. At the end, the waiter poured out two glasses of a rich claret and left them.

Angela raised her glass to the handsome man across the table. "Well, he was right about most things, but he never told me about your sense of humour, Peter."

"He?" The vampire regarded her over the rim of his glass. Wine and eyes caught the light of the candle on the table. Both glowed crimson.

"My employer. The man who wants you dead. Completely dead, that is." She sipped at her wine. "You have made an awful lot of enemies over the years, you know."

"Ah, revenge." He said the word without rancour. "A husband? Lover? Parent?" He shrugged. "Wife? Ah, but no. You said 'he', didn't you?"

"I think that is best left unanswered. Call it professional courtesy."

"Professional?"

"Oh yes. You see, Peter, we have a lot in common." Angela leaned forward and lowered her voice. "We're both killers."

The waiter arrived with the first course.

By mutual consent, the diners postponed further talk of business. "This is another surprise, you know," Angela said. "The food I mean. I'd always thought you took everything you needed from," and she allowed her eye to follow the waiter, "other sources."

"You confuse survival with pleasure," said the vampire, unfurling a napkin. "The two are not always the same."

It was well over an hour later that the waiter finally cleared away the remains of an excellent meal, and the vampire and the woman were once again left undisturbed to enjoy their coffee and brandies. "So, Angela," he said, leaning back in his chair and swirling his brandy in its balloon glass, "do you always introduce yourself to your potential victims before you dispatch them?"

"No. But then you are so very different from any of my previous assignments." Angela leaned forward. "You'll have to forgive me for being so blunt, Peter, but I confess that I find you very attractive."

"Of course you do."

"I don't mean that. Vampire hypnosis is far too well-documented for me to leave myself unprepared for it."

"I prefer to think of it as unusually strong charisma."

"Whatever." She gave a dismissive wave of her hand. "What I'm saying is, I was attracted to you long before I'd even heard the name Peter Weston." She sank back in her chair, her finger tracing lazy circles around the rim of her glass as she regarded him. "Or any of the many other names you've used over the years." She abruptly raised the glass to her lips and threw back its contents in one go, replacing it firmly on the table and looking up at the vampire with burning eyes. "I want you to make love to me, Peter."

For the count of several seconds the vampire met the intensity of her gaze. In the end, it was he who looked away. "And what makes you think I can?" he said quietly.

She laughed again. "You eat, you drink, and you smoke. What's left to do?" She leaned forward, much further this time, and her voice lowered almost to a hiss.

"And the legends *reek* of it!" Her tone changed again, becoming almost bantering. "Even the movies make it explicit these days."

The vampire's response came slowly, as if he was carefully weighing every word. "Yes. You are of course correct. I can make love to you. I might even *want* to make love to you. But tell me, Angela," and he placed his own glass back down on the table, "Why should I? Why shouldn't I just kill you here and now, take your hot, sweet blood, and rid myself of the potentially dangerous embarrassment that you represent?"

Around them, the other diners continued their meals. Waiters glided silently to meet their needs. The room was filled with the subdued murmuring of polite table talk. Looking at the man and the woman, a casual observer would have seen only an attractive, young couple, possibly married, probably not, enjoying the benefits of their money. The casual observer would not have sensed the charge in the air when hunters meet and recognise that the slightest slip will determine which of them is the predator and which the prey.

"You won't kill me," Angela said clearly. "Not here. Not now. Because you can't." The vampire arched an eyebrow. "Not in front of all these people. That's not how a vampire operates. You need the shadows, literally and metaphorically. You need the secrecy. You depend on people's doubt that you even exist for your own security, probably more now than at any time in the past." She smiled, an expression without a trace of warmth or humour. "And ripping my throat out in a five star hotel restaurant is just no guarantee of anonymity."

"So," the vampire replied with the calmness of a chess player countering an opponent's attack. "I take you outside. And I kill you there."

"I've already told you," she said with just a touch of impatience, "you can't 'take' me anywhere. But even if I let you, even if we walked out now together, arm in arm, and went straight to your room, even then there are a dozen ways I could destroy you before you could so much as extend those marvellous teeth of yours."

The vampire made a small moue of distaste. "Idle boasts?"

"Cold facts. This week alone there have been five separate occasions when I could have dispatched you without your even knowing I was near. But I didn't. You might even say that for that reason alone, you owe me."

The vampire pressed his hands together, almost as if in preparation for prayer, his eyes never moving from her face. "Fascinating," he murmured. "If I actually believed what you are saying . . . "

"What? What would you do, Peter, if you believed me?"

The vampire remained silent, and unblinking.

"Yes," she said. "It is time to stop talking." She held out her hand, the skin pale, the veins making pale blue traces on her wrist. "Take me to your room. Make love to me. If you dare."

"Fascinating," the vampire said again softly. He reached out and took her hand in his.

"So cold," she said.

Together they rose and left the restaurant.

In his room, he took the shawl from around her shoulders, allowing it to fall to the floor as he moved around to face her. She shivered once, but faced him, silent, expectant.

He took her in his arms, pulled her slowly towards him, lowered his head. He brushed her gently pulsing neck with his lips. She gave a short moan, choking off the sound almost as soon as it emerged. His lips moved down her throat, as with his hands he undid her dress, slid the material down her shoulders in a whisper of silk, and stroked the uncovered breasts. Her breath grew ragged at the chill pressure of his undead flesh on hers. It was she who pulled them both to the bed.

She clawed and bit at his cool, ivory skin, her teeth and nails leaving pale indentations in his resilient flesh, while he explored her eager body with his hands and with his mouth. With barely articulate cries she urged him on as he moved across her stomach, down her legs, back across the breasts, to return at long last to her neck. His mouth was burning ice that seared where it touched. Like an animal now, he was pushing into her neck, pushing, licking. And then she felt it, the twin hardness of cold teeth, the pressure of fangs against her throat. "No!"

Later, he would realise it had come from that hand purse, thrown with such apparent carelessness onto the bedside table. Now, all he could think of was the biting pain in the thin skin across his breastbone. Instinctively, he went to pull backwards and away, but her arm was around him pulling him back down to her, and to the ruthlessly simple weapon she held in her other hand.

"Oak, mistletoe or rowan, I don't know, and I don't think it really matters." She was breathing heavily, her face flushed, but the weapon in her fist didn't move. "This is just over nine inches of sharpened wood, a stake by anyone's definition, and I'll bet that's enough to cool anyone's ardour." She shifted her body slightly to one side so that he could see. "So, what's it to be?" She pressed, just a little pressure, and one round drop of gelid blood oozed with unnatural slowness from the vampire's skin.

For the first time in a very great number of years, the vampire's control was lost to an overwhelming surge of instinct. When he drove into her, she screamed like a child then laughed wildly as she threw her arms around him and demanded still more. The stake fell with a clatter back to the bedside table, forgotten.

* * *

The early morning sun filtered through the hotel bedroom curtains and dappled the prone forms lying side-by-side on the twisted sheets. It was Angela who opened her eyes first and turned her head to regard the man next to her. The vampire lay there with his eyes closed, quite still. It was the first time she consciously noted that he did not breathe. She reached out a finger and traced a light line down his unmoving chest. The tiny wound caused by her stake had already disappeared. "Would you crumble into dust if I ripped open the curtains and let the sun in?" she whispered.

"Probably not," he replied immediately and clearly, "though it might give me the devil of a headache."

She laughed and leant across him to reach for her purse. She felt the muscles of his body tense beneath her. "Smoke?" she said, holding up the two cigarettes she had retrieved and her silver lighter.

"You really do have everything in there don't you?"

"Oh, you'd be amazed." She lit the first cigarette, drew on it then passed it to him before lighting the other. She allowed herself to fall back into her pillow and for a moment the two of them shared the silence and the mellow smoke.

"Well," said the vampire eventually, "at the risk of sounding like a callow adolescent, which I assure you is a state I left behind a long, long time ago, how was it for you?"

"What?" Angela snorted with incredulous laughter. "Is this the giddy heights of vampire pillow talk?"

The vampire propped himself up on one arm but seemed unmoved by her reaction. "No, I'm genuinely curious. You have spent an evening making love to a man who, by all the accepted medical definitions of the day, is quite dead. How did it feel? Was it what you expected?"

Angela looked up at the ceiling and breathed out a long stream of smoke. "No," she said finally. "No, it wasn't."

"Oh."

She laughed out loud and rolled over onto her stomach, looking sideways at him. "And that was what made it so bloody marvelous."

"Ah. Pride salvaged. My dear, you gave me quite a nasty moment there."

"So I saw. Men and vampires aren't so very different it seems." She drew on her cigarette. "The next question is usually, 'where do we go from here'."

"No." The vampire moved closer, sliding one arm under her body so that she was almost cradled next to him. "My next question is, why?"

"Christ!" Angela's eyes suddenly blazed with unexpected anger. "You really are just like ordinary men aren't you? You don't *listen!*"

"I don't . . . "

"No, no, of course you don't. Well listen to this and perhaps you will. I went to bed with you, with a dead man, to remind myself that I'm still alive. Do you understand that?"

The vampire was silent for a moment, then, "No," he said.

Angela swore loudly. "No," she mimicked. "Well, think. Yes, it was weird getting off with you. Yes, it was scary not knowing what the hell was actually going to happen. And that's what made it so *good*." Something of the fire went out of her then and he felt her body, that had become so rigid with anger, loosen once more. "Like it used to be," she concluded wearily, "before it all got so boring, so quickly. Like the killing was, before that got boring, too."

"You kill because you are bored?"

The surprise in his voice made her turn to look at him again, and she saw something in his face that she hadn't seen yet: genuine puzzlement. That and something more, a reaction she couldn't readily identify. But it was unexpected, and that excited her. More, it was like a glimpse of vulnerability where she had least expected to find it. She knew she had to make him understand. "I'm talking about challenge and about *sensation*, can you understand? About walking up to the unknown, reaching out and taking it by the throat. About living on the edge. I have to have that feeling. I need it, or I'm as good as dead. Walking around, but dead."

"Like me?"

"No, not like you." She pulled him closer to herself, lay her flushed cheeks on his cool, white chest. "You're not dead, not inside where it counts. I was pretty sure of it before we met, and then when we talked at dinner. But do you know when I was really sure?" He was silent, and she continued almost without pause. "When I pulled that stake on you. I could have killed you then. You knew that, and you liked it. Didn't you?"

The answer, when it came, was almost a whisper. "Yes."

"Just like me. Excited by the unexpected, by the

danger. Two of a kind."

She closed her eyes and for a moment, he thought she'd fallen asleep again until he felt her hand stroking the smooth, flat muscles of his stomach. "So, what does come next?" he said. "Are you going to kill me now?"

She laughed, kissing his ribs, then his chest and stomach. "No. Not now. I was going to, I admit it, until I got to know you. I mean, really know you. But not now."

"What about your . . . contract?"

"Screw the contract! If the old goat makes a fuss, I'll kill him." A shadow flickered deep within the vampire's eyes but was gone before she noticed it. "For the first time in my whole life, I think I actually know what I want."

"And what is that?"

She threw herself on top of him, eyes sparkling, her voice like an excited child's. "Make me a vampire. Let me be with you. Together, we can show humans and vampires what dull, pathetic creatures they all are. Do it to me! Do it now!"

He lay beneath her, looking up. "And when you become bored with that?"

"I won't. How could I? As a vampire I'll be even freer to do anything I want than I am now. Forever."

"Freer?" He shook his head, his expression almost sad. "We're no freer than you are. The body may die, but the heart, the conscience, they live on."

"I'm being lectured on morality by a vampire!" She took his head in her hands, pulled his face close to hers, her breath warm on his cheek. "You're talking about guilt, but people like you and me don't need guilt. It's for the slow people, the stupid people. I can show you how to do away with it, how to cast it off like an old skin. Peter, let it go, and I can make you feel like you felt tonight again and again, and again." Without warning she arched her body up and backwards, thrusting her hips hard against his. "Wouldn't you like that, Peter? Wouldn't you?"

"Yes." With one swift motion he rolled her over so that it was he who was astride her. She gave a small scream of pleasure and didn't resist. She lay there, arms wide, vulnerable, and hungry. "Yes, I would dearly like that," he said.

"Then do it." She tilted her head back and closed her eyes. "Do it!"

She never even saw the stake the vampire had recovered from the table as it arced down and slammed between her breasts and into her heart.

"You are extraordinary," he said with genuine pain in his voice, "but you really are far too much of a monster to become a vampire."

He cradled her head until it was over and he could soothe away the look of incredulous agony from her face.

* * *

Two days later. Another country. Another restaurant. And yet, the vampire thought, depressingly similar to all the other restaurants in which he had spent so much of his unlife. He didn't even look up as the silver-haired man approached his table, pulled out a chair and sat down. "You took your time," the new arrival said without preamble.

"The job was done as specified. You didn't stipulate a time limit."

The old man cleared his throat, but did not look displeased. "Yes, indeed. It certainly was. Papers were full of it. Didn't expect it to be so messy though."

"Things . . . didn't go quite according to plan."

"Oh?" A look of alarm briefly crossed the old man's face. "Did she suspect?"

"That you'd set her up? That the only reason you'd hired her to kill me was to make it easier for me to kill her? " The vampire paused, lengthening the old man's discomfort. When he spoke again, he did not bother to hide his contempt. "No, she didn't. And if she had, it would hardly have made any difference, would it?"

"No, no, I suppose it wouldn't." The old man coughed nervously. "Still, all's well now, eh? The bitch that killed my son is dead, my wife and I get to put the past behind us, and you got to enjoy yourself a little, and . . ."

The vampire's head snapped up. His eyes were chips of ice. "I do what I do for survival, not for pleasure."

"Ah yes, quite," the old man fingered his collar unconsciously, snatching his hand away when he realised what he was doing. "And as to that, the money has been paid directly into your account, so . . . "

"That's not what I meant!"

"Ah, no. Of course. I'm sorry."

The vampire closed his eyes. His voice flattened, lost its fire. "There is no need to apologise. It is a distinction that others have also failed to recognise." He took a cigarette from the packet on the table.

"Ah, light?" said the old man, with a pathetic eagerness to please.

"Thank you, no." The vampire extracted a lighter from his jacket, a flat block of silver and held it up to catch the light. "Beautiful, isn't it?" he said softly, stroking it gently with his fingers.

Amalthea
Terrie Leigh Relf

His each and every gaze
the flow of blood
beneath glacial ice
a shattering of stars
as I call out
delicate palms

soles still stained
an august hue
scent of cinnamon,
cassia, henna
so many hearts
within canopic jars
when at your birth
I was as a ruby hidden
memento mori
pomegranate seeds
upon my tongue
to welcome rebirth
as midwives
reach into my darkness
reveal this gateway
to the stars
and when at last
your birth
not with a caul
but opalescent cords
about your neck
red
all was red
and so we welcome
you, Amalthea,
into our arms
darkness into our bed.

Lost Dreams Bookshop
By James W. Bullard

The old bookshop has been around before people can remember. An aging caretaker is finally being replaced and the new manager realizes the shop itself is sentient. The bookshop survives by deriving energy from its patron's lost dreams and uses that energy to manipulate people. A series of barely interacting victims who have shopped in the store over the years are telepathically summoned to return to the shop and gather on a single day not realizing their fate is in the hands of the sentient shop.

James W. Bullard lives in Colorado with his girlfriend, his son, and a spoiled Aussie shepherd. Writing is a hobby along with watercolor painting and drinking craft beer.

Type: Novella
Audience: adults

Ordering Links:
Print Edition ($10.95):
https://www.hiraethsffh.com/product-page/lost-bookshop-by-james-w-bullard
ePub Edition ($3.99):
https://www.hiraethsffh.com/product-page/lost-dreams-bookshop-by-james-w-bullard
PDF Edition ($3.99):
https://www.hiraethsffh.com/product-page/lost-dreams-bookstore-by-james-w-bullard